87.

The Song
of the
Christmas
Mouse

The Song of the Christmas Mouse

by Shirley Rousseau Murphy
drawings by Donna Diamond

HARPER & ROW, PUBLISHERS

Library of Congress Cataloging-in-Publication Data
Murphy, Shirley Rousseau.
  The song of the Christmas mouse / by Shirley Rousseau Murphy ;
drawings by Donna Diamond.
      p.   cm.
  Summary: Rick's efforts at capturing a beautiful wild mouse for a
pet seem constantly thwarted by his willful younger cousin who has
come to stay for Christmas.
    ISBN 0-06-024357-0 : $ — ISBN 0-06-024358-9 (lib. bdg.) :
$
  [1. Mice—Fiction.   2. Christmas—Fiction.   3. Cousins—Fiction.]
I. Diamond, Donna, ill.   II. Title.
PZ7.M956So 1990   89-19744
[Fic]—dc20   CIP
                                                            AC

Typography by David Saylor
1 2 3 4 5 6 7 8 9 10
First Edition

Contents

The Song
of the
Christmas
Mouse

Chapter 1

HUNGRY

The mouse had a den in the woodpile, a hole between the split logs. Her walls were lined with pine needles and dry grass. Her bed was the dog-chewed foot of a sweatsock. Long ago, her mother had dragged the old sock there. The little mouse liked to sleep inside it. Her mother was gone now. All the food her mother had stored in the den was gone.

She didn't know her mother was dead, or where her three brothers were. They were just not there anymore.

She woke from sleep very hungry. Sitting up, she washed her pointed face. Carefully, she smoothed her pale

whiskers. She was too hungry to sleep anymore, too hungry to play. Her den was cold. She could smell the freezing cold from outside. She sniffed the empty nest, making little squeaking, comforting sounds to herself.

She wasn't gray like a wild mouse, nor

white like her mother. She was all curving stripes and splotches, gray and white, rich as silk. Her eyes were large and dark, her ears so thin the light shone through.

Days ago, she found a few scraps of food in the garbage can behind the big house. But yesterday, when she went there, she couldn't get in. Thick ice held the lid shut. In the woods and yard all the ground was frozen, locking away the roots. Many seeds were frozen into patches of ice.

She made a high, unhappy squeak. Painfully hungry, she pushed through the door of her nest, into a crust of snow that covered the woodpile. She dug wildly.

She broke through, sending a spray of snow shooting out. She stood under the vast, open sky.

Snow clung to the woodpile. Snow clung to the sides of the big house. But the ground between was bare, the lawn frozen to dead brown.

The little mouse reared up in the icy air. Her tiny paws waved. Her whiskers twitched as she sniffed.

It was early evening, shadows gathering. It would be dark soon. Birds sped by, hurrying for a last meal before roosting. Owls were coming out to hunt. The little mouse quivered, but no owl saw her. Her silver-and-white coat seemed part of the shadowed snow.

Soon the scent of cooking drew her down off the woodpile. She stood on the spiky, frozen lawn, facing the big house boldly. The smell of food made her shiver.

She knew where food could be found, high up the house wall. It was dangerous to go there. But she was too hungry to care.

She stared up at the sky.

Nothing flew above her.

The little mouse sped across the brown grass. Every puddle was a sheet of ice. She reached the house. It was huge, a mountain above her. The basement window was high off the ground. With sharp claws, she scrabbled up the rough brick wall. Atop the basement window, she stood shivering.

Then she leaped from window to rose trellis.

Up she climbed, dodging thorns, toward the bird feeder attached to the kitchen window.

When she jumped from trellis to feeder, birds exploded away, squawking.

Two wrens landed again, scolding her. The blue jay settled. He was big enough to eat her: When he dove at her, she ran, heart pounding. Escaping his beating wings, she squeezed into a nook between trellis and feeder. He couldn't reach her. There she hid, watching him. And watching the reflections of moving birds in the window.

Suddenly, a huge pale shape stirred behind the glass. The jay screamed, the birds swept away in panic. The terrified mouse streaked to the edge.

She looked down. She turned to stare at the glass. When the figure moved again, she leaped away into space.

She dropped down and down, into a patch of leaves.

She lay dazed, her breath knocked out. But a sudden sound from the house made her jump up and race for the woodpile.

She pushed down through the snow to her hole, heart pounding.

Inside, the warm smell of her nest comforted her, the sharp smell of pine and of mouse. She snuggled down inside the sweatsock, shivering. She was very empty. She longed to go out again and look for food, but was too frightened.

It was later, and snowing, when she heard something big clumping around the woodpile. She huddled deeper into the sock, her dark eyes huge with fear.

Chapter 2

SEARCHING

Rick stood at the kitchen window, puzzled. What had he seen racing across the
feeder? The birds had exploded away when
they had seen him, the jay screaming.

But something else had been there.

A mouse? That was crazy. Why would
a mouse be on the bird feeder? And who'd
ever seen a mouse that color?

He'd been looking out at the sky, hop-
ing for snow. It had snowed a few days
ago, but not enough for sledding. He'd
waited two months, his new sled hanging
unused. And tomorrow was the first day
of Christmas vacation. A wasted vacation,

without snow. Then, when he had moved, the birds had leaped away. And something pale had flashed across the feeder, disappearing in a blur over the side.

It was as small as a mouse, but striped gray and white. A strange, tiny animal.

He closed his eyes, trying to bring it back in instant replay. Gray-and-white curvy streaks. Long pale whiskers. A long thin tail. It sure had looked like a mouse. But its coat was patterned like ripple ice cream.

He pressed his face against the glass, searching the yard. It must have been pretty hungry, to be on the bird feeder. And leaping off—that was a jump of over twelve feet. He slipped through the back door to look. The wind cut like ice through his shirt.

He found a dent in the snow where the little animal had fallen. Its tiny tracks led away. Excited, he followed. The wind howled around the corner. He could hear

Sandy snuffling and whining in the house. He didn't let her out. Sandy was a yellow Labrador. Retrievers weren't supposed to catch mice, but who knew what Sandy would do?

He lost the tracks where the snow ended; he stared around the yard. With the wind blowing every leaf, who could

see a mouse move? It would be hiding now—from the wind, and from him. Even his white mouse, Lucy, had hidden from him when she had escaped from her cage.

Lucy had gotten out of her cage just before Halloween. They had tried to lure her back, but no luck. They hadn't seen her again—until two weeks ago. The neighbor's cat had her. Dad got her away from the cat, but it was too late. Lucy was dead.

"She's had babies, though." Dad had shown Rick. She had been nursing them.

They had buried Lucy under the red holly bush, in a box that Mom covered with chintz. They searched a long time for her babies, but couldn't find them.

"They'll die," Rick had said.

"They would be good-sized," Dad said. "Her milk was drying up. I think they would have started to feed themselves. If she had food stored in the nest, they could live. I'll bet Lucy was a good mother—I'll bet she had plenty of seeds and roots put away."

"And maybe some of our garbage," Rick said, remembering chewed papers around the garbage can.

"Yes," Mom said. "A mouse could get in under the dented lid. And Lucy was smart. She must have been a good mother."

Lucy had known seven tricks and would come when Rick called her. Except that one time, when she got out into the world.

It was getting dark, and colder. He hoped for snow before morning. Deep and perfect, covering Barker's Hill.

He searched for the mouse until it was too dark to see. His ears felt like ice cubes. Mom thought he was in his room, reading. He could hear Sandy scratching at the back door. Suddenly, it began to snow. Fast, hard flakes. He stood in the driveway letting it cover his face, laughing, jumping up and down. "Snow! Snow all night! Let it snow forever!" Already it was dusting the grass. He did cartwheels, stood on his head.

When he went in, he was numb with cold. Sandy greeted him leaping and licking as if he'd been gone for years. He knelt, hugging her, pushing his face against her to get warm. Mom was shouting for him. He dripped across the linoleum, his thoughts filled with snow.

"What were you doing? Come get warm—and wipe up the water. The floor looks like a lake." Mom handed him a rag.

He stood dripping, shivering. "A mouse, Mom—a really terrific mouse."

She stared at him. "In the snow?"

"Before it started snowing. It was right outside the window, on the feeder." Rick knelt, wiping up water. "It jumped down and ran. I found its footprints. It was really strange. Silver and white—like ripple ice cream. I lost its trail."

Mom went to the window, staring out.

She was tall, her pale hair pulled back and tied with red yarn. There was a smear of flour on her cheek and across the front of her red sweatshirt. "I've never heard of a mouse like ripple ice cream."

"Parfait ripple—silver parfait ripple."

She grinned, shook her head. "A silver parfait ripple mouse."

"You don't believe me."

"Well . . . put some food out—maybe it'll come back. If I see it, I'll believe it. And take a hot shower; you're freezing. Then get your clothes out of your room. Your aunt and cousin will be here after dinner. I've already changed the sheets."

Rick groaned. His cousin Hattie Lou was a pain. "If I can catch the mouse, I can keep it in Lucy's cage—teach it to ride on my shoulder the way Lucy did."

"And make nests in your hair the way Lucy did."

Rick grinned. Lucy's nest making used to tickle his head. He went to move his clothes, thinking of the parfait mouse sitting on his head, like Lucy.

He dug his ski pants and boots and a sweater out of his closet. He had already moved his models and fishing gear to the basement, away from seven-year-old Hattie Lou. She and Aunt Claire would have his room until after Christmas. He didn't mind sleeping on the couch, but Hattie Lou wasn't getting into his things again this year. He hated his room after they were gone. Aunt Claire always left it smelling like perfume.

He put his clothes in the hall closet. The snow blew at the window, sticking to it. He meant to be the first on Barker's Hill. He could feel the red Canadian Blazer flying down the unmarked snow.

It had taken him a year of paper-route money to buy the big new sled. It hung in the garage, bright red, its silver runners waxed and ready.

Now that it was snowing, life was perfect.

Except, Hattie Lou was going to scream up a storm demanding to use his new sled. She'd been visiting them when he bought it. "You'll let me ride it, won't you Ricky? I'll get to ride your new sled when I come at Christmas, won't I?"

He'd told her *no. No way.*

But he knew Hattie Lou. She made everyone miserable until she got what she wanted.

He slammed the closet door. In the morning, he'd be out of here before the little pest woke up. Even if he had to wait in the dark up on Barker's Hill. She wasn't using his sled. She could play with his old sled, in the yard.

Chapter 3

A MOUSE?

Dinner was beef stew and corn bread. The kitchen table faced the window. Snow whirled against the glass, fast in the streaming light.

Rick opened the window, brushed snow from the feeder, and put some corn bread down. "I hope it snows all night, covers everything—cars, houses."

Dad blew a gust of breath white into the icy blast. "Feeding the owls?"

"Mouse," Mom said. "Corn bread for the mouse."

Rick's father leaned back, giving her a lopsided grin. "Mouse? On the bird feeder?"

Rick nodded. "Mouse." He stared out at the corn bread. "Maybe I should have put butter on." He opened the window again, smeared on butter.

Dad's silence challenged him. A veterinarian, Rick's father knew a lot about animals. "In the middle of winter? On the feeder? A *mouse*, Rick?"

"A mouse. *I swear!*"

"Have to be pretty hungry to climb up there. Expose itself to the owls, to the wind. . . ."

"A gray-and-white-striped mouse. Gray-and-white ripples."

"Ripples?" Dad kept a straight face. But Rick could see his amusement. He thought Rick was putting him on.

"Silver," Rick said. "Silver—ripples."

Silence.

"I saw it! I'm not making a joke. I swear I saw it!"

"Maybe a flying squirrel, streaked with snow?"

"Smaller than a flying squirrel. Skinny tail, no fur on it. And it wasn't snowing yet." Rick looked steadily at his father. "I saw its footprints, too, where it fell in the snow. A mouse. But smaller than Lucy. A little silver ripple mouse."

Dad nodded, so solemn Rick couldn't see any hidden grin. "There *are* striped mice in Africa. Tree mice. An exotic pet dealer might have one. But there are no dealers like that around here. And none of my clients has a striped mouse. I'd have heard about it."

It was snowing harder. Sandy pushed her golden head against Rick's knee, begging. Rick said, "Could the mouse be Lucy's baby? Some kind of crossbreed, if she mated with a wild gray mouse? We never found her babies."

"Have to be a pretty unusual crossbreed—white ancestors in the wild male. Take several generations of crossing.

You'd get spotted mice before you got a striped one."

"White ancestors? Oh," he said, disappointed. "A wild mouse wouldn't have white ancestors."

"It could. You're not the only kid whose white mouse escaped and went wild. There's been a pet store in town for years—generations of kids have had white mice."

Mom said, "I lost three white mice when I was your age, down on Park Street. They got out when I was cleaning their cage. Don't you remember—I told you about them, when Lucy ran away."

"Oh, yeah."

After Lucy escaped, Mom said that maybe the little mouse had longed to be free. That maybe Rick should be happy for her. But then when the cat got her, Mom felt really bad.

Now Rick said, "I'm going to catch that

mouse. I can use the humane trap." He had bought it to trap Lucy, but then the cat got her. A humane trap wouldn't hurt an animal. The door would slam closed when the mouse went in for food.

Mom said, "If we had trapped Lucy, she would never have found a mate and had babies. I think Lucy must have relished those few weeks of freedom."

"I know," Rick said. "But if Lucy had a silver-and-white baby, I bet she'd like me to take care of it. It's pretty cold out—the wind's pretty strong and icy."

After dinner, Rick brushed snow off the corn bread on the feeder, but it was soon covered again. He guessed the mouse would smell it. Maybe it wouldn't come until morning. He'd put out a fresh piece before he went sledding. Sandy stood barking at him, maybe jealous because he was putting out food for another animal.

Aunt Claire and Hattie Lou arrived late and tired. The driving had been slow, the traffic heavy. Hattie Lou was stocky, with yellow hair and blue eyes. She was sleepy now, and cross. She began playing with the Christmas figures Mom had put on the sideboard.

While Mom fixed sandwiches and cocoa, Rick foolishly opened the window to dust snow off the corn bread. That started Aunt Claire asking questions. Mom shot him a look. He should have known better. Stumbling, he tried to explain.

Aunt Claire looked appalled. "*A mouse?* You're feeding *a mouse?*" Aunt Claire had a thing about animals.

Sandy came into the kitchen. Hattie Lou held her sandwich over her head, where the retriever couldn't reach. Sandy thought she was going to throw it, and began to bark.

Aunt Claire said, "How *could* you feed a mouse? You'll have the filthy creatures all over! No one wants—"

Mom interrupted. "It's just one little mouse, Claire. A rare and unusual one— a striped mouse. It isn't coming inside. It can't come through a closed window."

Hattie Lou stared up at the window, her eyes widening. At seven, Hattie Lou was into magic. "If it's a rare mouse, maybe it's enchanted. Maybe it *can* come through a closed window." She shivered. "But I hope not. No one wants a creepy mouse in the kitchen—even a magic one."

Chapter 4

HATTIE LOU

Everyone stared at the closed window, picturing a mouse coming through.

"Anyway," Hattie Lou said, "whoever heard of a striped mouse? Maybe its hair's falling out, maybe it has a disease. I thought you were done with mice, Ricky, after that awful white mouse you had last summer—the one the cat ate. . . ."

Rick wanted to smack her.

Hattie Lou knew he was angry, but didn't back off. Instead she slid closer to him. She was a pushy kid, nervy. "You'll wake me in the morning, won't you, Ricky? So I can go sledding with you?"

He didn't answer.

"Of course he will," Mom said.

Rick's turn. He gave Mom a withering
look.

Dad came in the back door with a load
of firewood. Hattie Lou was saying, "And
I can ride your new sled, can't I, Ricky? I
can ride the big red sled!"

Rick clenched his jaw, but kept silent.

"It's Christmas," Hattie Lou said. "I'm company. Of course I can ride your new sled."

"You're not company. You're my cousin."

Dad said, "We cleaned up Rick's old sled, Hattie Lou, polished and painted it. The new sled's too big. If it got away from you, you could hurt yourself."

"I know how to ride a sled."

Aunt Claire sighed. "Mind your manners."

"I only want to ride it a little while."

Yeah, Rick thought—like all the first day of good snow. He'd been told not to fight with her, that that only made her worse. He'd like to whack her. One thing led to another, until Aunt Claire sent Hattie Lou to bed. Sandy followed, and when Rick heard Hattie Lou scream, he knew Sandy had licked her face.

Mom told Rick to call his dog. Rick and Sandy went out to the garage to dust off his sled, and see if the runners needed wax.

Chapter 5

THE TRAP

The Canadian Blazer shone red and silver in the garage light. Rick stood admiring it. But suddenly he imagined Hattie Lou trying to pull it down off the wall.

He didn't have a lock. He found a piece of heavy wire. He wound it around a runner and to a spike in the wall, twisting it tight, with pliers. No seven-year-old was going to unwind that. As he put away the pliers, he heard a soft, scurrying sound. He turned, silent, searching the shadows.

He shone his flashlight into the shelves. No mouse. No little bright eyes. Then he saw mouse footprints in the dust on a low shelf, near his sled. It must have been right here, right beside him.

He searched for the mouse behind paint cans and in corners, knowing it wouldn't let him find it. Then he got the ladder, and the humane trap from a top shelf. He went back in the house and spread a piece of bread with peanut butter.

In the garage again, he baited the trap and set it on the low shelf. He put in some rags for warm bedding, so the mouse wouldn't freeze.

Rick woke at midnight, his covers half off the couch. Sandy was asleep at the other end, hogging the thick quilt. He stared out through the living-room windows. It was still snowing hard. The Canadian Blazer was the best sled he could have bought. It was going to turn on a dime—do the obstacle course on Barker's Hill faster and better than anyone ever had.

He went to the kitchen to see if the corn bread was gone. It was covered with snow, and soggy.

Maybe he'd already caught the mouse. Maybe she was in the humane trap right now, eating the bread and peanut butter. He thought of going out to the garage. Instead, he crawled back under the warm covers, shoving his feet under Sandy.

He'd check the trap in the morning. He could get the mouse settled in Lucy's old cage and still be the first one on Barker's Hill. He thought of the mouse as *her*, like Lucy.

Maybe he should set his alarm. But he wouldn't need it. His folks were always up by six—pitch dark in the winter. He'd be gone before Hattie Lou woke. She never got up before sunrise.

He slept soundly. Much later, he didn't feel Sandy leave the couch. He didn't hear the back door open, then close softly.

Chapter 6

CAUGHT

It snowed all night, sticking to trees and roofs and piling up on parked cars. Snow covered the woodpile. The mouse den was cozy beneath its thick blanket.

But the mouse was not in her den. She was running along the shelves in the garage.

She ate some spilled grass seed, but couldn't get into the metal container. When the garage door had opened earlier, she had frozen with fear. Rick's huge shape had filled the space, and she had darted into a corner.

The boy had come and gone, making a lot of racket. She had fled from him each time, shivering, hiding. But then at last the garage was silent again.

And there was a new smell, wonderful. She leaped down the shelves, toward the peanut butter.

The wire cage frightened her. Circling it, she sniffed. Her whiskers wiggled with the rich scent of peanut butter. Her tongue came out, tasting the smell. Her little paws gripped the wire.

But then she backed off. The trap was too strange.

Very hungry, she crept out into the night, heading for the bird feeder.

Speeding through the silently falling snow, she leaped up the brick wall to the top of the basement window. Up the trellis she fled, bellyflopping onto the snowy feeder.

She could smell food under the snow. She crouched, staring up at the reflecting window.

When nothing moved in the glass, she

sniffed the snow. She dug, kicking up a shower of white. Uncovering the corn bread, she squeaked with pleasure.

She ate it all, in hasty nibbles.

She licked up the crumbs with her pink tongue.

There was still an empty place inside

her, but only a small one. Every crumb gone, she raised her nose to the sky.

In the still night, the little mouse made a squeak of happiness—a trilling cry as clear and piercing as the cry of a bird. It was a song, a trembling mouse song.

Her song of pleasure filled the snowy night. She sang for a long time, warmed by good food. She was happy. Then, her song finished, the little mouse sat washing her paws and whiskers.

Done with her grooming, feeling strong now, she leaped down and sped across the snow toward the woodpile. She was beside the garage when she smelled the peanut butter again. That little empty corner in her tummy guided her. She swerved in.

She crept toward the food. She was bold now, fed and warm. She circled the trap, then pushed at it. She tried to slip in underneath. She leaped to the top, trying to reach down inside. She circled again, pushing at the bars.

When a wall gave way, she reared back, hesitating. Then, brazen, she pushed. She was in. The door slammed behind her. She spun, stared at it. Then she approached the bread.

She circled it, sniffed. Then she ate, quickly and neatly, licking peanut butter from her whiskers. When the food was gone, she tried to get out.

She couldn't. The wall wouldn't push. She ran up and down the cage walls pushing, battering at them, trying to force her way through.

Chapter 7

THE SLED

In bed, Hattie Lou waited, pretending sleep. When she heard her mother's slow, even breathing, she slipped out. She was very quiet. In the kitchen, in the tool drawer, she found a flashlight.

Back in the bedroom she laid out her snowsuit and boots, her gloves and cap, and the flashlight. She set the alarm clock, hiding it under her pillow. She climbed in beside her mother, smiled, and fell asleep.

The next morning, Hattie Lou was up and dressed before anyone else woke. Slipping down the hall, she looked into the living room. Yes, Rick was asleep. She went quietly through the kitchen to the back door.

Sandy heard her. The retriever slid off the couch, following her to the kitchen. Hattie Lou, afraid Sandy would bark, gave her half a loaf of bread.

As Sandy ate, Hattie Lou slipped out. It was snowing hard, snow swirling in the beam of the flashlight. She forced her way through the deep, soft drifts toward the garage.

Inside the house, Sandy finished the bread and pressed against the door, whining. When Rick's mother got up and came in to start breakfast, she saw the bread wrapper. She scolded Sandy and let the retriever out.

In the garage, Hattie Lou shone her flashlight on the Canadian Blazer. Red and silver, it shone back at her. Next to it hung Ricky's little old sled. It looked battered even if it did have new paint. Hattie Lou found a box, and stood on it to lift the Blazer down.

It was wired to a spike in the wall.

She hunted for the pliers. Finding them at last, she began to untwist the wire. It was wound tight, very stiff. She grew cold and cross. As she fought the wire, Sandy came in out of the snow. She stood in the door, watching. She didn't bark—she was too sad from being scolded. Hattie Lou didn't see her, nor did she look into the dark shelves. She was sweating and mad by the time she got the wire off.

It took all her strength to lift the sled down. Staggering, she banged her ankle so hard tears came.

When Sandy saw Hattie Lou staggering with the sled—like a huge stick—she barked sharply. That scared Hattie Lou. She swung off-balance with the heavy sled, falling against the shelves. The sled hit the mouse cage. The cage fell on its corner, twisting open. As Hattie Lou sprawled

under the sled, hurting, the terrified mouse leaped out, shooting across her legs.

Hattie Lou bit back a scream. The mouse was small, and kind of pretty. But what did she care about a mouse? She was mad at Sandy for scaring her, and mad at the sled for being wired to the wall. As she pulled herself out from under the sled,

Sandy came to lick her. Hattie Lou let out all her anger by hitting the retriever, hard. Then she grabbed the sled rope and dragged the Canadian Blazer into the night.

Swinging her flashlight, she headed through the snowfall for Barker's Hill.

Sandy stood looking after her, puzzled and hurt, then went back to the house, where she could smell breakfast cooking.

Chapter 8

NOT A NIGHT BIRD

Mom set a plate of pancakes and bacon in front of Rick. Dad was already eating. It was surgery morning; he went early for surgery. Rick and Dad wolfed their breakfasts down, not talking, passing the butter and syrup back and forth. While they ate, Mom let Sandy in, wiping the snow off the Labrador's feet. When Mom spread a piece of pancake with bacon fat and syrup, Sandy looked hopeful. But Mom opened the window and laid the pancake on the snow. Shutting the window, she wiped snow off the inside of the sill.

Dad was through eating first. He pushed back his chair, hugged Mom, reached for

his coat. It was barely light. They stood looking out the window where the pancake lay atop the snow. He said, teasing her, "Not many mice get pancakes for breakfast."

Mom grinned, and hugged him back.

Rick said, "I set the humane trap last night."

Dad nodded. "I don't like to see wild things caged. But we did it when we were kids."

"I won't keep her long. Just until spring, until it's warm."

"Her?" Dad asked.

"Like Lucy."

Mom said, "I thought—I dreamed I heard its little voice in the night."

Dad frowned. "I heard something, too. Something woke me—a squeaking. It didn't sound like a night bird."

Mom said, "It sounded more like a tiny animal than a bird. But it *was* a kind of song. A bright, shrill little cry."

"A song?" Rick said, laughing.

"Possible," Dad said. "There've been such cases reported. One mouse sang when it heard radio music."

But Rick was thinking about the cry of fear. He grabbed his coat and headed for the garage. If she was in the trap, she was safe.

Chapter 9

BARKER'S HILL

Rick burst through the garage door wondering why it was open. The humane trap lay on its side, one corner broken, the bread gone. There were mouse droppings, but no mouse.

Had a cat gotten in, tipped the cage over?

He looked for blood, and for a hurt mouse.

When he rose and turned, he saw the empty wall. The Canadian Blazer was gone. He stood staring at the empty space.

Hattie Lou! He called her names he wasn't supposed to say, then ran into the falling snow.

He found fast-disappearing tracks: small boots, big runners. She was headed for Barker's Hill. He followed. It was snowing harder. When the tracks disappeared, he ran straight for the hill.

The five blocks of town were silent and dark. Barker's Hill rose beyond the post office. In the summer, it was a pasture for calves. Every winter, after the calves were sold, Mr. Barker piled a stack of straw at the bottom of the hill against the barbed wire fence. When snow had covered it, it made a good stopping hill.

Above on the hill, five stands of pecan trees broke the run. That was the obstacle course. Not hard to dodge, if you were skilled. Off to the left the hill was clear— for the little kids. Rick passed the post office and climbed the snow-covered fence. There was no trail of small boots and runners. But his own trail was fast disappearing.

He expected to see Hattie Lou at the

top of the hill, ready to take off.

There was no one.

Then he saw, halfway down the hill among the trees, a lumpy heap. He saw a silver runner, a smear of red.

He started running. He reached the heap and began to brush away snow.

Hattie Lou lay twisted in a runner. She was icy cold, shaking with silent sobs. Her leg shouldn't have been bent in that direction.

He tried to keep his voice soft. He guessed her leg was broken, and that it must hurt pretty badly. He felt sorry for her. But also he thought she deserved what she had gotten. Because of her, his sled was only good for firewood. "Hattie Lou?"

She didn't answer.

"Hattie Lou?"

"Go away!"

"I think your leg is broken."

She stared, scowling, her eyes red and

swollen. He had to give her credit. She wasn't whimpering.

"I'll get someone." He pulled off his jacket and scarf and covered her. He ran skidding down the hill, looking for help.

Nothing was open. The police station must be. He ran the five blocks to it, his lungs burning.

The patrol car sped back, Rick in front beside Sergeant Summers, siren blasting.

They climbed the hill and knelt over Hattie Lou. The sergeant slipped the sled and runner away from her leg. He slit her ski pants with his knife, looked at her twisted leg.

"Break off a splint from that wood, Rick."

The sergeant bound Hattie Lou's leg with a red slat from the Canadian Blazer. The child didn't cry. Maybe she was too cold.

Soon Hattie Lou was in the emergency room of the town hospital. She lay on a table, covered with blankets. Mom and Aunt Claire hovered as the doctor set her leg. When he pulled it straight, tears streamed from Hattie Lou's eyes. But she didn't scream.

An hour later, Hattie Lou was hobbling out in a white cast, enjoying the attention. She was more like herself now. Talkative. No one said she shouldn't have taken Rick's sled. No one said they were sorry Rick's new sled was ruined. But Mom's look, and her arm around Rick, said it.

Mom drove Hattie Lou and Aunt Claire home, while Rick went back for his sled. There were kids on the hill now.

"Rick! Hey, Rick—what happened? Your sled . . ."

"Hey, Rick . . . wait up!"

He turned away from their shouts. Alone, he gathered up the remains of the Canadian Blazer and started home.

Chapter 10

SORRY?

At home, Rick laid his sled out on the garage floor. He stood staring down at the twisted metal and broken wood.

A whole year delivering papers! Getting up in the middle of the night. Biking across town in the rain and out on muddy country lanes, trying to keep his papers dry.

He'd like to pound his stupid cousin. Why had he bothered to bring the sled home at all? It was nothing but kindling. He wanted to punch something, throw things, break windows.

He stared at the Canadian Blazer.

He began to wonder if he could fix it.

The runners would have to be heated, to straighten them. There was a welding shop the other side of town. Even then, they might never be the same.

The broken wood could be replaced. He wasn't much of a carpenter, but he could try. The slats were bolted to the metal frame. He'd have to get the right kind of wood, dry and strong. Have to drill it, sand and paint it.

He turned from the sled, thinking how hard he'd worked to buy it. He stared at the broken cage, wondering where the mouse was. Maybe she was hurt. Or dead.

He searched for her among the boxes and cans, feeling worse and worse. He saw no blood. He got some food, made a nest, in case she was hurt and couldn't get to her own nest. Then, filled with black thoughts, he took his old sled down, shouted for Sandy, and headed for Barker's Hill.

When he and Sandy got home it was nearly dark. They were both wet and starved. Rick was hoarse from yelling. His anger was gone. Mom had a pot roast in the oven.

There was a fire in the fireplace. Hattie Lou was sitting on the couch, on Rick's blankets. Her cast was propped up on the coffee table, her crutch beside it. Her fairy-tale books were scattered around her. Rick wanted to ask her what happened to the mouse.

Hattie Lou wouldn't look at him. She kept looking down, ashamed. He'd never seen her ashamed.

In a tiny voice, she said, "I'm sorry, Ricky."

But when she looked up, Rick could see the anger in her eyes, and knew she'd been told to say it. He didn't need that kind of apology. He turned away, went to wash.

Hattie Lou hobbled to the bathroom door and stood looking at him.

"Go away, I'm washing."

She held out something in her fist.

He thought for a sick minute it was the mouse. But she wouldn't hold a mouse.

"It's my allowance. Momma said—she gave me my allowance for the next year. She said—she said . . ."

"What happened to the mouse, Hattie

Lou? What did you do to the mouse?"

She just stared at him.

"What did you do to it?"

"Nothing! I didn't hurt it. It ran away. Take the money," she shouted. "I have to give it to you!"

He pushed her fist back and shut the door.

"I didn't hurt your stupid mouse!" she shouted through the door. "The money's to pay for a new sled!" He heard coins rattle on the hardwood, heard her stumping away.

When he opened the door, coins and bills covered the floor. He stepped over them and went to dinner.

Chapter 11

MOUSE CIRCUS?

It was Mom who picked up the money and made Rick take it. "As much for Hattie Lou as for yourself. It's a lesson she needs to learn."

He wished Hattie Lou could learn a lesson about animals—about creatures smaller than she was. He didn't believe she hadn't hurt the mouse.

He put the money in his dresser. There probably wasn't another Canadian Blazer in town, even if he wanted it.

After dinner, Rick and Dad took the runners off Rick's sled and measured for new boards. They made a list of what they'd need. Then Rick got to work on the humane trap. He pounded it back into shape with the sledgehammer against a wooden block. He wired up the torn corner. He was still working on it when Dad went in the house.

The next time he looked up, Hattie Lou was standing in the doorway. Leaning on her crutch, she watched him.

"What do you want, Hattie Lou?"

"To help you fix your sled."

"We already have it apart. What could *you* do?"

"Hold things. I want to help you fix it. I want to help you set the trap again."

"Why don't you just go in the house and mind your own business?"

She started to cry.

"Come on, Hattie Lou." He turned a box on end and helped her sit down. She sat cradling her crutch like a doll, staring at him, sobbing.

"You can help bait the trap," he said.

She reached in her pocket, handed him a warm cooky. "They're baking the Christmas cookies."

"You should be coloring the icing."

"In a while. I want to help you first. Ricky?"

"Yes?" He put the cooky in the trap. He had already put in the warm bedding. "Hold the door up. That's right."

"Ricky—it *is* a pretty mouse."

He stared at her. "You saw it."

"I told you—when it ran. It *was* pretty."

Rick put the trap on the floor near the hole.

"Ricky?"

"What is it, Hattie Lou?"

"Where does the mouse live?"

"I don't know. In a hole somewhere. Maybe in the garage."

"Doesn't the mouse get cold at night?"

"Mice put bedding in, to keep warm. Straw and rags and stuff."

"Ricky?"

"Yes, Hattie Lou."

"It was really, really pretty. Pretty

enough to be a *circus* mouse. You could have a *mouse circus*!"

"A mouse circus? That's the stupidest idea I ever—"

Or was it?

She was bawling again. He put his arms around her. "Maybe it isn't such a bad idea. Maybe, Hattie Lou—maybe it's a great idea!"

She looked up at him, beaming.

Chapter 12

DESSERT FIRST

The next morning, Rick was in the kitchen before Mom. Sandy knew he was going sledding, and was wagging and pressing against him. He'd just make a sandwich and some cocoa, and they'd be gone. He could hear Mom showering. He started to turn on the light, but first went to look at the feeder. He had left a whole banquet last night.

The food was still there. He'd just leave the light off, and maybe the mouse would come. He started drinking his cocoa by the light from the hall. Mom came in. She glanced at the feeder, and at Rick. She didn't turn on the light. She started some oatmeal. They kept looking out the window.

Mom had stirred the oatmeal twice when she touched Rick's arm. The trellis leaves were trembling. Something was moving there.

The leaves shook. A tiny creature leaped to the feeder.

The little mouse was there. So suddenly that Rick couldn't believe it. She reared

up, watching the sky. There was just enough light to see her against the snow. They didn't dare breathe.

She turned, looked directly at the window. She lifted her paw, shivering. Her gray streaks were all curves and splotches. Her tail was pale pink, striped with gray. Her long whiskers were white. Her eyes were huge, dark, and shining in her tiny, striped face.

When nothing moved in the glass, she picked up a crumb of cake in her paws and began to nibble. Lucy had eaten like that, holding her food in her paws.

Mom whispered, "She's eating her dessert first."

They watched her nibble her way through cake, then ham, then potato. She ate one thing at a time. Finished, she washed her face and paws, staring around her for danger.

They heard Hattie Lou stump from the carpet onto the linoleum. Before they could stop her, the light flared on, reflecting in the mouse's eyes. She streaked into the rose trellis and was gone. Rick whirled to scowl at Hattie Lou.

"I'm sorry, Ricky. I didn't know— Was the mouse really there?"

"She was," Mom said, hugging Rick. "And she was beautiful."

Hattie Lou said, "I wish I'd seen her, too."

Disgusted, Rick pulled on his jacket. Mom said, "Not without breakfast."

Mom dished up oatmeal and poured cocoa for them both. "You can decorate the cookies today, Hattie Lou. You do such pretty ones."

They always trimmed the tree on Christmas Eve, with decorated cookies in the shapes of stars and bells and angels, and wise men and animals. Their family had done it this way ever since Rick's great-great-grandfather was a child.

"Before I decorate the cookies," Hattie

Lou said, "I have to make a tent and a blanket for the mouse."

"Oh?"

"When Ricky catches it, it's going to be a circus mouse. I need some scraps of cloth to sew a tent for it to live in, and to make a blanket for its bed."

Rick looked at Mom. Mom looked at Rick.

Hattie Lou said, "Maybe we can have a whole circus of mice. Jumping through burning hoops. Walking a tightrope on their hind legs. *Famous* circus mice. And rich women will buy them for a lot of money, and keep them in silver cages. Then we'll all be rich."

When they were alone, Mom said, "What got into her?"

"I don't know," Rick said. "I think I liked her better when she left me and my animals alone. I hope she doesn't get any more crazy ideas."

Chapter 13

DESTRUCTION

When Rick got home from sledding, Hattie Lou was digging in the woodpile.

She had pulled firewood out, scattered it all around her. Hattie Lou sat in the middle, her broken leg propped on a log.

"What are you doing? Does your mother know you're out here?" He saw a chewed sweatsock, then the chewed-up litter that mice make.

The mouse nest?

"What are you doing!" he shouted. *"What have you done!"*

"I found the nest! Look!" She held up the sweat sock.

Rick wanted badly to hit her. He felt

like bawling. The mouse would never come back. It would be lost in the snow, die without a home. Be eaten by an owl before it ever found a new home.

"Why did you do that! You've killed it!"

"I went to look in the trap. In the garage. I found the mouse footprints, coming here."

"And so you tore up its home! What did you think you were going to do? Catch it with your bare hands?"

Hattie Lou's eyes were big and hurt. "I was going to bring the trap here. After I found out where the nest was, I was going to set the trap here."

"You thought the mouse would *come back? After you tore up its house?*" He was so mad, he didn't think he dared stay near her. He turned and ran.

He didn't even have his own room to be alone in.

He went to the garage.

She didn't come after him.

Sandy did, licking him and whining. He was so mad he couldn't even hug her.

After a long time, he decided to put the woodpile and mouse nest back together. Probably wouldn't do any good. But he could put the sweatsock back in, and the grass, and pile the firewood above it.

But when he got to the woodpile, it *was*

back together. Not a trace of the sweat sock.

Hattie Lou had gone. He could see the marks of her crutch and cast, and her handprints in the snow.

Rick stared at the snow beside her handprints.

There were mouse prints!

Fresh mouse prints! Going over the top of Hattie Lou's prints!

Going into the nest?

He didn't believe it.

And there were no prints coming out.

He backed away. The mouse was in there. He just didn't believe it.

To be safe, he got the humane trap from the garage and hid it in the house. He didn't want Hattie Lou to set it by the woodpile. If the mouse got caught outdoors, it could freeze to death before morning.

Chapter 14

COOKY TRAIL

Hattie Lou sat at the kitchen table tying ribbons through holes in the bright cookies. It was early Christmas Eve. Dad had come home at noon, and he and Rick had gone up the mountain. Rick had picked out a tree and cut it. They had hauled it down, Sandy careening around them. It stood in the living room now, bare and smelling of pine, waiting to be decorated.

After dinner Dad built a fire, and Mom put Christmas records on. Aunt Claire cut the fruitcake. Rick and Dad hung the tiny tree lights and silver rope from the branches.

The most important part was hanging the cookies on the tree. There were wise men with robes of red and purple icing. Animals with gold glitter, and bells with silver glitter. The angels were all white icing. The room smelled of fresh cookies and fresh pine. Sandy ran around like a puppy until Dad made her settle down.

It was hard for Hattie Lou to move around, with her cast on. She sat on the couch telling everyone where to hang each

angel, each shepherd, each bell. Last, they put on other decorations, thin silver bells that tinkled, and silver balls that caught the light. Then they had cocoa and fruitcake, and sang, and listened to carolers out on the snowy street.

When they were ready for bed, Hattie Lou decided to sleep in the living room. "Just like Ricky. Near the tree."

Rick said, "It gets too cold in here. The floor's hard."

"I'll bring the mattress and blankets."

"But . . ."

Mom said, "It's Christmas Eve, Rick."

Dad brought Hattie Lou's mattress and blankets, and Aunt Claire got her settled. Hattie Lou put her mouse blanket and tent beside her pillow. The blanket looked all right, but the tent kept collapsing.

Long after the Christmas tree lights were out, Hattie Lou was wide-awake. She wouldn't stop talking. Rick pretended to go to sleep. He lay ignoring her, watching the dying coals. She wanted to know what he did in school this year. She wanted to know why he let Sandy sleep on the couch. She had a hundred questions. At last she stopped and drifted off to sleep. Rick sighed, glad to enjoy the decorated tree in silence. With Hattie Lou asleep, the room seemed his again, private.

Moonlight, reflected from the snow, made the room silver-white. The glittering cookies and ornaments shone. It was the most beautiful tree he could remember. He decided to sleep beside the tree every Christmas. He lay thinking.

He was about to get up when Mom slipped in with an armload of presents. She knelt to arrange them under the tree. Rick smiled. At last she tiptoed away.

Rick got up, and got the trap from the hall closet.

He put a leftover cooky in, and took the trap to the kitchen. He meant to set it out on the bird feeder, check it every few hours. But he might oversleep. The mouse could freeze.

He took the trap back in the living room.

He put it on the carpet between the living room and the kitchen. It was far away from Hattie Lou, but he could see it from the couch.

He went back to the kitchen and opened the window. He laid a few cooky crumbs across the feeder and propped the window open with a jar lid. He put a crumb inside on the sill, and two crumbs on the kitchen counter. He set a kitchen chair up to the counter so she wouldn't have so far to jump, and put a crumb on the seat. He laid a few crumbs across the kitchen floor leading into the living room. He didn't want too many. He wanted the mouse to be hungry when she found the trap.

He got Sandy's leash and tied her to the couch leg. She could still climb up with him, but she couldn't reach the cooky trail.

Chapter 15

THE CHRISTMAS MOUSE

It was nearly midnight when the little mouse ran across the crusted snow. She climbed to the feeder and began to nibble crumbs. They were small, far apart. She ate her way quickly to the window.

There she paused. The open window was different, alarming. She stretched out toward the cooky smell.

She drew back three times before she flashed under. She snatched the food and swerved out. Safe again in the snow, she ate.

She crept back to the window. There was more food in there. She trembled, hesitated. At last she crossed under again.

This time, she stood inside on the sill, rearing and waving her paws. There were good smells here. And it was warm.

In the silence, when nothing moved, she jumped to the kitchen counter. She ate the crumbs, then sidled to the edge. Her whiskers twitched. Nothing stirred. She jumped to the chair, ate the small crumb. Soon she was following the cooky trail across the kitchen floor. No one saw. The dog and children slept soundly.

The little mouse stopped at the living-room carpet. She touched it, puzzled by the thick pile. Then she hopped up onto it, stood up on her hind legs to look around.

The room was full of smells. Dog. People. Dinner, fruitcake, cocoa. But mostly the sweet cooky smell. And the smell of fresh pine, pleasing her, for it was like her nest.

She ate all the crumbs on the carpet, then circled the trap. She remembered it.

Afraid, she turned away, toward the safe smell of pine, and the smell of cookies.

She flashed to the tree and burrowed among the presents.

She popped out again, ran over packages, twitching her nose. She touched a silver bow. Then she leaped to the trunk, and climbed. She was soon hidden among the branches.

She moved lightly along a branch, across ornaments and silver rope. A cooky dangled from the branch above. She bit off a piece, coating her whiskers with crumbs.

She ate all of that cooky that she could reach. Then she moved to another. And another. Each time she moved, the silver ornaments flashed. Their movement excited her. Shivering, she paused to watch their dancing light.

Her eyes were like two dark jewels. She reached a paw toward a glittering ball. When she touched it, it swung. She raced away.

She touched another ornament, then ran from it, flicking her tail.

She touched a velvet ribbon. It felt soft as mouse fur, and she licked it.

She brushed by a silver bell. It tinkled, startling her, so she fled. But the bright sound excited her, too. She returned to it, touched it again. When it rang, she squeaked at it, then whirled away.

She sped along the moonlit branches. She jumped over silver rope, racing higher up the tree. At the top, the moonlight was brightest. She grew very still. Above her hung the gleaming star, caught in moonlight.

She looked and looked at the star. Then she squeaked out a long, trilling cry.

Wildly, down she raced.

Up and down she ran, leaping from branch to branch, excited by the glitter and the moonlight. And, racing, she trilled her high clear cry. A mouse song, clear as bells.

Rick woke up.

The whole room looked silver. The Christmas tree seemed made of silver light.

Something was moving in the tree, shaking the silver bells, making the light leap. And there was the song, high and trembling.

A tiny creature raced up and down. Rick thought he was dreaming. He watched the ornaments swing, listened to the tiny song.

Then he saw the little creature herself flashing along the branches.

He saw her pause.

He could see her whiskers moving. He could see her dark eyes flashing, her paws waving. He glanced at Hattie Lou. She was sleeping. The mouse whirled away, racing on. Her high little song rose and trembled. Madly she ran, making silver chains swing.

She's *playing*, Rick thought. She's singing and playing, among the ornaments and lights.

Suddenly she stopped.

She turned, one paw raised.

She was looking at Rick. Staring right at him.

Her eyes gleamed, huge in that tiny face. She sat perfectly still, looking at him. And Rick knew, in that instant, her pure joy—in the moonlight and in the wonder of the bright tree—and in her freedom to race through it uncaged.

When he glanced at Hattie Lou—not turning his head or moving—he saw that she was awake. He was sure she'd move or shout. But Hattie Lou did not. She was still. And there was a look on her face he'd never seen.

The mouse darted away, up the branches. Rick and Hattie Lou watched. She stormed up the tree to just beneath the star. There her bright song filled the room.

Then the mouse left the tree. She scurried down, and fled past Rick, past the trap, to the kitchen. He heard the scrabble of her feet across the counter, then silence. She would be back on the snow-covered feeder.

After a while, Hattie Lou got onto the couch with him, snuggling down. Neither one said anything.

In the morning when he woke, before presents, before opening his Christmas stocking, Rick looked closely at the tree.

He saw the half-eaten cookies, the drooping silver rope, the fallen bells.

He took the cooky out of the humane trap. Hattie Lou was quiet, didn't say a word.

It was very early. When they had put the cage away, Hattie Lou pulled on her boots and coat over her pajamas. She went out into the snowy morning carrying her mouse blanket. Rick watched through the window as she crossed the silent snow.

She took her mouse blanket to the woodpile. There, she knelt and laid the tiny blanket by the mouse hole. She stayed still a minute, whispering something.

When she came in, she pressed close to Rick, hugging him. He hugged her back, feeling the coldness of her coat and face. She said, "No mouse circus."

"No. No mouse circus."

"No cage," she said.

"No cage."

Hattie Lou looked up at him. "She's a magic mouse." She took off her coat and boots and got into her bed, smiling.

Rick heard his folks getting up, heard the shower, then the coffeepot start. He sat on the couch, still seeing the little mouse racing through the bright tree.

He didn't know how to tell his folks what he had seen, how to make them believe he hadn't dreamed it.

When Mom and Dad came into the living room, they stood with Rick and Hattie Lou, looking at the crooked ornaments and the dangling silver rope and half-eaten cookies. Rick showed them some tiny tooth marks in the icing of a cooky. And together Rick and Hattie Lou began telling them what they had seen, interrupting each other. They tried to make them see the little Christmas mouse leaping up the light-filled tree jingling the bells, eating the cookies, and singing her high, clear song.